TRAVEL LOG

HUH-HUH

Written by Kristofor Brown
Beavis and Butt-Head created by Mike Judge

books

MTV Books / Pocket Books

Beavis and Butt-head are not role models. They're not even human.
They're cartoons. Some of the things they do would cause a real person to get hurt,
expelled, arrested, possibly deported.
To put it another way: don't try this at home.

Beavis and Butt-head created by Mike Judge
Art Direction/Reiner Design: Roger Gorman and Leah Sherman
Art Director/MTV: Vicky Smith
Senior Art Supervisor: Dominie Mahl
Writer: Kristofor Brown
Editor: Dave Stern
Production Manager: Sara Duffy
Illustrators: Mike Judge, Mike Baez, Nick DeMayo, Brian Moyer, Bryon Moore, Sue
Perrotto, Bill Moore
Production Assistant: Brent Thorn
Cel Painter: Lisa Klein
Background Painter: Bill Long

Special Thanks: Eduardo A. Braniff, Andrea Labate, Brad MacDonald,
Kim Noone, Ed Paparo, Renee Presser, Robin Silverman, Donald Silvey, Monica
Smith, Jen Stipcich, Machi Tantillo, Abby Terkuhle, Van Toffler,
and James D Wood

Special thanks at Pocket Books to: Lynda Castillo, Gina Centrello,
Lisa Feuer, Max Greenhut, Donna O'Neill, Liate Stehlik and Kara Welsh.
Also thanks to Al Travison at Stevenson and Paula Trotto.

This book is a work of fiction. Names, characters, places, and incidents are either
products of the author's imagination or are used fictitiously.

An Original Publication of MTV Books/Pocket Books

POCKET BOOKS, a division of Simon and Schuster, Inc.
1230 Avenue of the Americas, New York NY 10020

Photo credits: Associated Press/Wide World Photos pp. 9, 14, 18, 25, 40, 44, 47, 55,
89; The Image Bank pp. 9, 22, 25, 27, 33, 56, 75, 82, 88, 95; Archive/Foto International
pp. 10, 23, 63, 85, 88, 92; Photofest pp. 10, 21, 50; Everett Collection pp. 11, 19, 26, 30,
32, 38, 40, 42, 43, 48, 49, 56, 57,
59, 64, 67, 70, 72, 75, 77, 80, 85; Archive/Reuters pp. 12, 17, 63;
Retna Ltd. pp. 15, 34, 53; H. Armstrong Roberts, Inc. pp. 22, 26, 34, 36, 60, 95; Duomo
Photography p. 33; Paula Trotto p. 35; Impact Visuals/David Rae Morris p. 51; Bettman
Archive pp. 59, 61; MTV Publicity pp. 90, 91;
Impact Visuals/Harvey Finkle p. 95.

ISBN: 0-671-01533-8

First MTV Books/Pocket Books trade paperback printing December 1997

10 9 8 7 6 5 4 3 2 1

Why You Should Go Somewhere

WHILE FILMING OUR MOVIE, 'BEAVIS AND BUTT-HEAD DO AMERICA,--AND WRITING OUR BOOK, 'HUH HUH FOR HOLLYWOOD,-- ME AND BEAVIS GOT TO TRAVEL ACROSS THIS GREAT LAND OF OURS. THAT'S RIGHT, THE UHHHHH... UNITED STATES OF AMERICA.

YEAH, HEH HEH. AND THIS COUNTRY'S REALLY BIG AND STUFF. IT COULD TAKE LIKE, A WEEK TO SEE IT ALL, AND THERE'S PROBABLY LIKE, UM, A HUNDRED THINGS TO DO. HEH HEH.

YEAH. AND NOW THAT WE'RE KNOWLEDGEABLE AND STUFF, SOME BOOK COMPANY ASKED US TO MAKE A TRAVEL GUIDE SO YOU CAN PLAN YOUR NEXT TRIP AND KNOW WHAT TO DO OR SOMETHING.

BUT UM, THERE ARE STILL A LOT OF STATES THAT WE DON'T KNOW ANYTHING ABOUT.

YEAH. SO WE JUST LIKE, MADE IT UP. HUH HUH. HOPEFULLY YOU WON'T BE ABLE TO TELL THE DIFFERENCE. HUH HUH.

YEAH, YEAH! SO GET OFF THE DAMN COUCH AND GET YOUR LAZY ASS OUTSIDE, DAMMIT! HEH HEH HEH. AND THEN, LIKE, UM... GO SOME- WHERE. HEH HEH.

UH, CRAPPY TRAILS, OR SOMETHING,

Butt-Head   Beavis

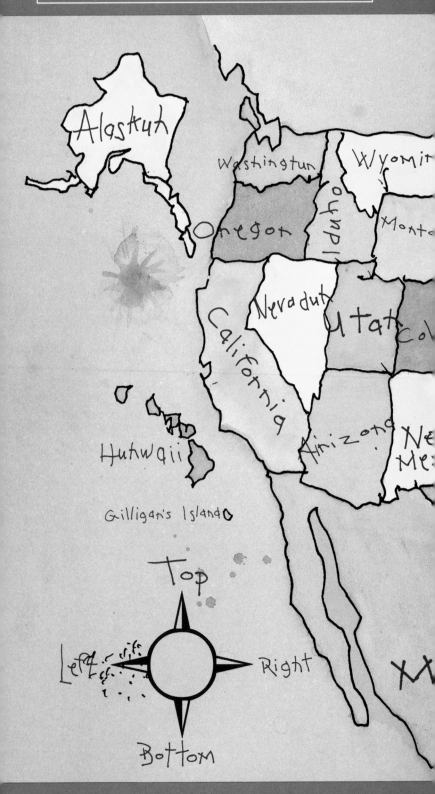

Alaskuh

Washingtun

Wyomin

Oregon

Idaho

Monta

Nevaduh

Utah

Col

California

Arizona

Ne
Me:

Hutwaii

Gilligan's Island

Top

Left

Right

Bottom

Canaduh

th Duhkota

uth Duhkota

hbraska

Kansass

Texass

:ico

Minnesota

Iowuh

Missouri

Oklukoma

Wisconsin

Illinoy

Arkansaw

Louisianuh

fishagen

Indiana

Kentucky

Misisipi

Ohio

Pensilvania

West Virginya

Tenesee

Alabauma

Greorjuh

New York

New Jerzey

Virginya

North Carolita

South Carolita

Flotiduh

Main

Vermont

New Hampsher

Massachusets

Read Island

Cometicut

Deluhware

Maryland

Washingtun D.C.

Vacation Tips
HOW TO PACK FOR YOUR TRIP

Porn.
IN CASE YOU WANNA DO SOME
SIGHT-SEEING. HUH HUH.

Condom.
DON'T LEAVE HOME
WITHOUT IT. HUH HUH.

Money.
UHHH... TO BUY MORE
CONDOMS.

TV guide.
TO REMIND
YOURSELF
WHAT YOU'RE
MISSING.

The BUFF

Nachos.
IN CASE YOU GET HUNGRY.

Rocks.
FOR, UM, SELF-DEFENSE.
HEH HEH. YEAH.

Dead mouse.
IT'S ALWAYS NICE TO
HAVE A PET ALONG.

Remote control.
IN CASE YOU GET BORED
WITH WHAT YOU'RE
LOOKING AT.

T.P.
FOR YOUR
BUNGHOLE.
HEH HEH.

Modes of Transportation

UHH, THERE ARE LIKE, A LOT OF DIFFERENT WAYS TO TRAVEL.

YEAH, BUT HOW SHOULD I CHOOSE? HEH HEH.

WELL, BEAVIS, I'M GLAD YOU ASKED. HUH HUH. PERHAPS WE SHOULD TAKE A CLOSER LOOK, OR SOMETHING:

- **Airplanes** are really dangerous. They're always crashing. Plus it's expensive to fly, so you might not only get killed, but you'll spend a lot of money, too. That sucks.

- **Trains** are dangerous, cuz they're moving really fast and you gotta jump into an open car. One time Beavis tried jumping on one of those kiddie trains at the zoo, but he slipped and fell on the tracks and almost got killed. Huh huh. What a dumbass.

- **Buses** suck. You can't just get on the bus and say, "Uhh, I wanna go to Seattle." I tried it once. But the bus driver told me to sit the hell down and then she drove me to school.

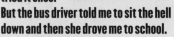

- If you have a **motorcycle** you can pretty much go anywhere and people are like, "Wow, you're cool. Are you in a band?"

- **Cars** are cool. Sometimes Todd takes me and Beavis in his car. But he always makes us ride in the trunk. Then he takes us out and kicks our asses.

- **Bikes** are cool for like, short trips to Maxi-Mart and stuff, but they make you exercise, so that sucks.

- **Horses** are cool, cuz you'll be going somewhere, and they'll just stop in the middle of the street to take a dump. Heh heh. Plop!

- **Walking** sucks, cuz it's really slow. But the cool thing about walking is it doesn't cost anything. Plus you can step on bugs and stuff.

- **Lawnmowers** rule. Sometimes me and Beavis take Anderson's lawnmower for a drive out on the street. Lawnmowers are kinda slow, but that's okay, cuz you can watch stuff fly out when you run it over.

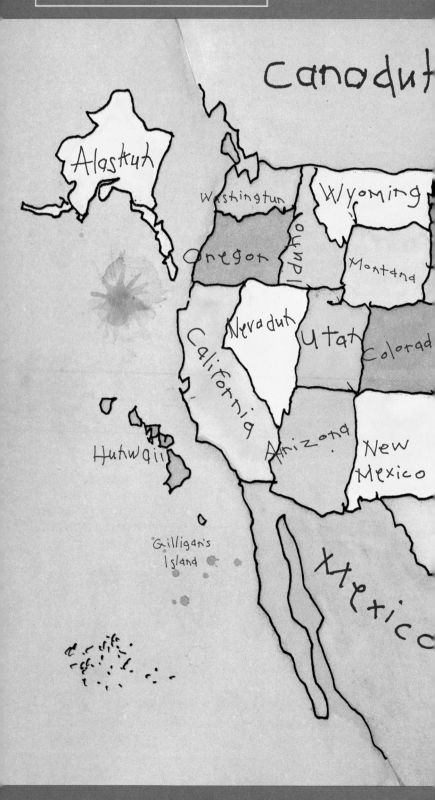

ALASKUH

Check it out, Alaskuh is like, the biggest state, but there's nothing here.

Yeah, really. It looks boring.

Uhhh... I guess they need ideas to fill it up.

Stuff they should put in Alaskuh to fill it up:

Some couches.

Naked chicks. This could also bring in a lot of tourists and stuff.

More parking lots.

A really big mini-mall.

A cool theme restaurant. Something like Porn Planet.

A demolition derby. Heh heh. With tanks and semi-trucks. Heh heh, yeah!

An explosion test site.

Nacho World Amusement Park.

The World's Biggest Porn Magazine.

Giant flesh-eating penguins.

Cool Town Names:
Chicken
Deadhorse
Livengood
Poorman
Marys Igloo
Pile Bay
Peters Creek
Twin Hills
Clam Gulch
Shaktoolik
Eek

THE ALASKUH PIPELINE!
HUH HUH HUH. PIPE.

HuHWAii

HEY BEAVIS, I HEARD THAT THE SECOND YOU GET TO HUHWAII, A CHICK COMES UP TO YOU, HOLDING SOME FLOWERS, AND YOU GET LAID. HUH HUH HUH.

WHOA, REALLY? YOU MEAN, YOU JUST DO IT RIGHT AWAY?

YEAH. HUH HUH.

SO, LIKE, WHAT ARE THE FLOWERS FOR?

UHHHH... I THINK YOU GIVE THEM BACK TO HER WHEN YOU'RE DONE.

YOU KNOW, TO BE ALL ROMANTIC AND STUFF.

HOW TO GET TO HUHWAII:

You hafta go to California and start surfing. But instead of going to the right, you go to the left.

Cool Town Names:
Napoopoo
Pepeekeo
Puu Waawaa Ranch
Hanapepe
Kapaau

CHECK IT OUT, THIS DUDE'S NAME IS DON HO. HUH HUH. HE'S COOL CUZ HE'S ALWAYS GETTING, YOU KNOW, LAID. HUH HUH HUH.

YEAH, HEH HEH. PLUS HE'S GOT A COOL LAST NAME.

GILLIGAN'S ISLAND

THESE PEOPLE ARE A BUNCH OF DUMBASSES. HUH HUH. IT'S LIKE, I CAN UNDERSTAND WHY THEY COULDN'T GET OFF THAT ISLAND AND STUFF, BUT LIKE, IF THAT PROFESSOR DUDE IS SO SMART, HOW COME HE COULDN'T FIGURE OUT THAT GINGER AND MARY ANN WANTED IT? HUH HUH HUH.

YEAH, REALLY. IF THE PROFESSOR WAS SO SMART, HE WOULD'VE KILLED GILLIGAN, THE SKIPPER, AND MR. HOWELL. HEH HEH. THEN HE WOULD'VE HAD THE CHICKS ALL TO HIMSELF. HEH HEH HEH.

YEAH, HUH HUH. HEY BEAVIS, WE SHOULD GO THERE. CUZ IF THOSE CHICKS ARE STILL THERE, THEY'RE PROBABLY REALLY HORNY BY NOW. HUH HUH HUH.

Cool Things to See

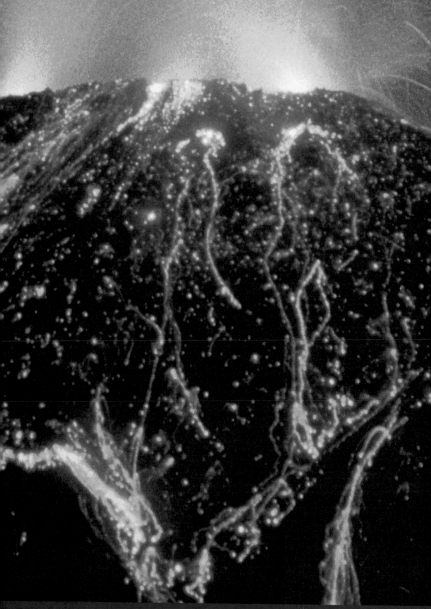

VOLCANOES

VOLCANOES KICK ASS. HUH HUH. THEY'RE LIKE, THESE GIANT FIRE-PUKING MOUNTAINS. AND THEY CAN MAKE YOUR VACATION UNFORGETTABLE OR SOMETHING.

YEAH, HEH HEH HEH! VOLCANOES PUKE OUT STUFF CALLED LAVA. AND IT LOOKS REALLY COOL, BUT IT'S REALLY HOT AND IT BURNS AND MELTS EVERYTHING IN ITS PATH, HEH HEH HEH! AND EVERYBODY STARTS RUNNING AROUND AND SCREAMING, AND PEOPLE SMASH THEIR CARS INTO EACH OTHER! AND IT RULES! HEH HEH. IT RULES!!! AAAGGGHHHH!!!

WHOA, HUH HUH. SETTLE DOWN, BEAVIS.

TAKING PICTURES

- Don't waste your film on boring stuff like nature.

- Take pictures of things you want to remember. Like chicks' butts. Huh huh.

- Zoom lenses make boobs and butts look bigger.

- If you're not sure how many pictures you have left, open the back of the camera and look at the film.

- Use Poleroyd cameras to take pictures of chicks. That way you can stare at the picture right away, without them knowing that you're still looking at them.

- Use disposable cameras. Cuz like, after you're done, you're just supposed to throw it away.

WASHINGTUN

Cool Town Names:
- **Humptulips**
- **Duckabush**
- **Fishtrap**
- **Packwood**
- **Bluestem**
- **Nooksack**
- **La Push**
- **Brief**
- **Relief**
- **Tumtum**
- **Mold**
- **Chuckanut Bay**
- **Battle Ground**
- **Walla Walla**
- **Wawawai**
- **Kooskooskie**

HEY BEAVIS, DO YOU KNOW WHAT "MICRO" MEANS?

UM, YEAH. IT MEANS LIKE, SMALL, RIGHT?

YEAH, HUH HUH. AND DO YOU KNOW WHAT "SOFT" MEANS?

UM... NOT HARD?

YEAH, HUH HUH. CHECK IT OUT, THIS DUDE MADE SOME COMPUTER STUFF AND HE NAMED IT AFTER SOMETHING THAT MEANS "SMALL" AND "NOT HARD." HUH HUH. WHAT A DUMBASS! HUH HUH HUH.

OREGON

Cool Town Names:
- **Wankers Corner**
- **Boring**
- **Butte Falls**
- **Lookingglass**
- **Remote**
- **Promise**
- **Sisters**
- **Sweet Home**
- **Friend**
- **Fox**
- **Bend**
- **Broadbent**
- **Burnt Woods**

WANKERS CORNER
CITY LIMITS

VERY LITTLE IS KNOWN ABOUT OREGON.

YEAH, HEH HEH. BY US. HEH HEH. BUT UM, WANKERS CORNER IS THERE. HEH HEH HEH.

BEAVIS, IF THERE EVER WAS A PLACE THAT YOU SHOULD VISIT, IT'S WANKERS CORNER. HUH HUH HUH.

YEAH, HEH HEH. THANKS.

Cool Cities – SEATTLE

SEATTLE ROCKS. IT'S LIKE, GOT ALL THESE COOL BANDS THERE AND IT RULES! HEH HEH.

YEAH, BUT IT ALWAYS RAINS THERE AND EVERYONE IS ALL DEPRESSED AND STUFF. SO THEY STAY INSIDE AND PLAY THAT DEPRESSING GRUNGE MUSIC. HUH HUH.

BUT THEN LIKE, ALL THOSE GRUNGE BANDS GOT FAMOUS AT THE SAME TIME AND THAT MADE THEM EVEN MORE DEPRESSED. HEH HEH.

YEAH, HUH HUH. AND NOW THAT GRUNGE ISN'T POPULAR ANYMORE, EVERY-ONE'S LIKE REALLY, REALLY DEPRESSED. HUH HUH.

SEATTLE NEEDS TO GO ON A VACATION OR SOMETHING. HEH HEH.

CALIFORNIA

The San Diego Zoo has over 4,000 animals. That means there's over 4,000 chances a day to see an animal taking a dump. Huh huh huh.

CALIFORNIA IS COOL, CUZ EVERYBODY LIVES ON THE BEACH AND THEY DRIVE REALLY COOL CARS.

YEAH. EVERYBODY'S RICH AND FAMOUS AND THERE ARE MOVIE STARS EVERYWHERE AND ALL THE CHICKS ARE REALLY HOT. HEH HEH.

YEAH. AND IF A CHICK ISN'T A MOVIE STAR, SHE'LL DO ANYTHING TO BECOME ONE. SO LIKE, A PRODUCER WILL TELL A CHICK THAT HE'LL PUT HER IN A MOVIE IF THEY DO IT. HUH HUH HUH. IT'S LIKE, A REALLY GOOD SYSTEM OR SOMETHING. HUH HUH.

AHH, BOY, THAT SOUNDS LIKE FUN. HEH HEH. IT'S A SHAME IT'S ALL GOING TO FALL INTO THE OCEAN SOME DAY. HEH HEH.

YEAH REALLY, HUH HUH.

T.V. AND MOVIE STARS USUALLY HAVE TO SPEND A LOT OF TIME IN COURT, AND IN LOS ANGELES THEY CAN STILL BE ON T.V. WHEN THEY'RE IN COURT. PLUS, GERALDO SAYS ANYONE WITH ENOUGH MONEY CAN GET OFF. HUH HUH HUH. BUT UH, THEY NEVER SHOW THAT PART. HUH HUH.

YEAH, HEH HEH. IT'S LIKE, THAT O.J. MOVIE WAS THE LONGEST MOVIE I'VE EVER SEEN.

BEAVIS, YOU DUMBASS. THAT WASN'T A MOVIE. IT WAS A MINI-SERIES.

WELL, WHATEVER IT WAS, I WOULD'VE NEVER GUESSED THE ENDING.

YEAH, REALLY. O.J.'S LUCKY HE DIDN'T GET THAT JUDGE WAPNER DUDE.

YEAH. WAPNER WOULD'VE SAID, "DAMMIT, O.J., YOUR STORY JUST DOESN'T MAKE ANY SENSE! NOW GO OUT IN THE HALL AND TALK TO DOUG LLEWELYN BEFORE I HAVE RUSTY THE BAILIFF KICK YOUR ASS!" HEH HEH HEH.

Cool Things to See

NATURAL DISASTERS
IN CALIFORNIA THERE'S ALWAYS COOL STUFF GOING ON THERE, LIKE
EARTHQUAKES, FIRES, FLOODS, MUDSLIDES, AND RIOTS. HEH HEH HEH.
YEAH, AND IT'S ALSO WHERE THEY FILM "BAYWATCH." HUH HUH HUH.

People You Should Visit

HUGH HEFNER

THIS IS LIKE, THE COOLEST OLD DUDE EVER. HE HAS THIS BIG MANSION WHERE HE KEEPS EVERY CHICK WHO WAS LIKE, EVER IN PLAYBOY. AND THEY'RE ALWAYS NAKED AND PLAYING IN THE POOL AND STUFF. HUH HUH.

YEAH, AND IF YOU'RE LIKE FRIENDS WITH THIS DUDE, HE'LL LET YOU COME OVER AND LOOK AT HIS MAGAZINES. HEH HEH HEH. BOOOOiiNNNG!

BEAVIS, YOU'RE NEVER GONNA SCORE. HUH HUH HUH. FARTKNOCKER.

DEATH VALLEY

DEATH VALLEY IS COOL, CUZ ANYTHING THAT GOES THERE, DIES. HUH HUH.

YEAH, REALLY. YOU SHOULD CHECK IT OUT. HEH HEH.

NO WAY. YOU SHOULD CHECK IT OUT. HUH HUH.

NO WAY. YOU SHOULD CHECK IT OUT. HEH HEH.

UHHHH... YOU FIRST. HUH HUH.

NO WAY. YOU FIRST.

UHHHH... WAIT A SECOND. I THINK OZZY LIVES THERE.

WHOA, REALLY? WE SHOULD GO THERE.

YEAH, HUH HUH.

Ozzy

Ozzy rules! Heh heh.

Yeah, huh huh. He's all rich and stuff now, so he can probably live wherever he wants. So like, he probably lives in Death Valley.

I bet if you like, showed up at his house with a dead animal or something, you know, to show you're cool, he'd probably invite you in and cook it for breakfast. Heh heh heh.

Yeah. He sure seems like a nice guy.

AiRiZONA

UHH, I THINK IT'S LIKE, REALLY HOT IN AiRIZONA. SO IF YOU GO THERE ON VACATION, HERE ARE SOME WAYS TO KEEP COOL:

- Pour a freezy whip over your head.
- Put your face up against a toilet bowl. No matter how hot it is, toilet bowls are always really cool. It's amazing. Heh heh.
- Hide out underground.
- Like, don't do anything. The less stuff you do, the less you sweat.
- Stand next to a freeway and let the wind from passing cars cool you off.
- Go to a Maxi-Mart and stand there with the freezer door open until the guy who works there gets pissed and threatens to call the cops.
- Go to another state with better weather.

NEW MEXiCO

UH, I THINK THIS IS S'POSED TO BE NEW MEXICO.

REALLY? IT DOESN'T LOOK THAT NEW.

YEAH, REALLY. WHAT A RIP-OFF. YOU'D THINK IF THEY WERE GOING TO GO THROUGH THE TROUBLE OF MAKING A NEW MEXICO THEY'D AT LEAST CLEAN UP ALL THE DIRT AND STUFF.

If you wanna see something cool, you should go to **Roswell, New Mexico**, cuz that's where all those aliens are always getting abducted.

Yeah. And you might get to see an anal probe. Heh heh.

PETRIFIED FOREST

CHECK IT OUT, PETRIFIED WOOD, HUH HUH HUH HUH HUH HUH!

YEAH, HEH HEH HEH HEH HEH!

HEY BEAVIS, THAT PARK RANGER DUDE SAID THIS WOOD GOT HARD CUZ OF SOME CHICK NAMED MOTHER NATURE. UH HUH HUH HUH.

WHOA. SHE SOUNDS LIKE A COOL MOM. HEH HEH HEH HEH.

YEAH. HUH HUH HUH HUH HUH.

NEVADUH

NEVADUH WAS BUILT IN THE MIDDLE OF THE DESERT AND THERE WAS LIKE, NOTHING TO DO AND EVERYONE WAS BORED. SO THEY LIKE, STARTED PLAYING CARDS. AND WHEN THE CHICKS LOST ALL THEIR MONEY, THE DUDES TOLD THEM THAT NOW THEY WERE GONNA PLAY STRIP POKER, HUH HUH. SO THEN THE GIRLS HAD TO GET ALL NAKED AND STUFF. HUH HUH. AND THEN THE GUYS WITH ALL THE MONEY GOT HORNY, SO THEY PAID THE CHICKS TO DO IT WITH THEM. AND THAT'S LIKE, HOW GAMBLING AND PROSTITUTION BECAME LEGAL OR SOMETHING. HUH HUH HUH. NEVADUH RULES.

Cool Cities – Las Vegas

Um, is this Las Vegas?

Uhhh... it kinda looks like New York.

Yeah. And check this one out, it looks like one of those peeramids from Egypt.

Oh yeah, huh huh. They must've won it like, in a game of poker.

Whoa. That's really smart. Cuz when they run out of ideas for new hotels and casinos, they just go to other cool places and play poker until they win the whole city. Then they move it out here.

Yeah, huh huh. Someday Las Vegas will have every single place that's cool. And like, you'll never have to go anywhere else. Huh huh huh.

Chicks. Huh huh huh.

SIEGFRIED AND ROY

CHECK IT OUT. HUH HUH HUH HUH HUH!

HEH HEH HEH HEH HEH! WHAT A COUPLE OF WUSSES! IT'S LIKE, THE ONLY
REASON THEY HAVE THAT TIGER IS TO PROTECT THEM SO MIKE TYSON WON'T COME AND
BITE THEIR REARS OFF. HEH HEH HEH.

BEAVIS, YOU DUMBASS. TYSON DOESN'T BITE PEOPLE'S REARS. HE BITES THEIR EARS.
HUH HUH.

OH, HEH HEH. CUZ I WAS GONNA SAY, THESE TWO GUYS LOOK LIKE THEY WOULDN'T
MIND HAVING HIM BITE THEIR REARS. HEH HEH HEH.

YEAH. IT'S LIKE, THESE GUYS DO MAGIC AND THEY'RE ALWAYS MAKING THAT TIGER DIS-
APPEAR AND STUFF. BUT LIKE, ONE OF THESE DAYS, THAT TIGER IS GONNA GET PISSED AND
HE'S GONNA EAT THEM AND MAKE THEM DISAPPEAR. HUH HUH HUH. IT'S GONNA BE COOL.

Vacation Tips

Hotel Guide

Hotels are cool, cuz you can like, get a room and put a glass up to the wall and listen to people in the next room doing it. Huh huh huh.

Yeah, heh heh. And you can take a dump in the toilet and somebody has to come in the next day and flush it. Heh heh heh.

Yeah, but don't waste your time at those crappy places called "bed and breakfasts." It's just a family trying to stick you in the basement and charge you for fruit and a croissant.

WHAT TO LOOK FOR:

- Places that say 'adult motel' with a lot of trucks out front

- Hourly rates

- Vibrating beds

- Free porn

- Doors that go directly outside so you can sneak chicks in and out, if you know what I mean, huh huh huh.

Um, Butt-Head, you've never snuck any chicks into a hotel room.

Yeah, but someday I will. Even if I have to pay for it. Huh huh huh.

Cool, heh heh. Then I'll get the room next door and listen to you. Heh heh heh.

National Parks

GRAND CANYON

The Grand Canyon is supposed to be a national treasure or something. But there's nothing to see anymore, cuz like, somebody must've come and dug up the treasure a long time ago.

Yeah, really. This place sucks. Now all there is is a big hole in the ground.

Hole, huh huh huh huh.

Ohhh yeah, heh heh heh.

MEXiCO Birthplace of Nachos

Mexico is the big state at the bottom where nachos come from and all the Mexicans live. So when you go to Mexico, it's cool if you know how to talk Mexican. Like, here's how to order nachos:

Placing the Order:
What To Say: YO QUIERO NACHOS, POR FAVOR. HEH HEH.
How To Say It: YO KYEH-RO NAH-CHOSE, POR FUH-VOR. HEH HEH.
Translation: I WANT NACHOS, PLEASE. HEH HEH.

Paying:
Mexican money is like, different than American money. So um, just keep giving them money until they tell you to stop.

Thanking:
What To Say: GRACIAS, SEÑOR.
How To Say It: GRAH-SEE-YAHS, SEEN-YOR.
Translation: THANKS, DUDE.

UTAH

UTAH IS THE HOME OF THE WINTER OLYMPICS OR SOMETHING. AND PEOPLE COME FROM ALL OVER THE WORLD TO LIKE, RUN AND SWIM AND ICE SKATE AND STUFF IN ORDER TO WIN JOBS ON TV COMMERCIALS.

ISN'T THAT WHERE THAT ONE CHICK HIT THE OTHER CHICK IN THE KNEE WITH A LEAD PIPE?

YEAH. HUH HUH. BUT SHE DIDN'T GET ANY COMMERCIALS, SO SHE WENT AND DID SOME PORN. HUH HUH.

THE OLYMPICS ARE COOL.

Cool Town Names:
Big Rock Candy Mountain
Devils Slide
Fry Canyon
Virgin
Ticaboo
Shivwits
Tooele

CHECK IT OUT, HEH HEH, DONNY AND MARIE. THOSE TWO ARE DUMBASSES. HEH HEH.

THEY AREN'T DUMBASSES, DUMBASS. THEY'RE MORONS. IT'S LIKE SOME DUDE ON T.V. SAID, 'UTAH IS FULL OF MORONS.

WHOA, REALLY? HEH HEH. I MEAN, IT'S NICE THAT THEY HAVE SOMEPLACE TO GO, BUT IT'S NOT SOMETHING I'D WANT TO BRAG ABOUT. HEH HEH.

IDUHO

POTATOES ARE LIKE, THESE THINGS THAT GROW IN THE GROUND AND LOOK LIKE TURDS. HEH HEH. AND UM, HERE ARE SOME COOL THINGS YOU CAN DO WITH POTATOES:

- Put one in your pants and tell chicks it's all natural. Heh heh. Oh, um, make sure you put it in the front of your pants. Yeah, heh heh.

- Put two of them together and pretend you're kicking Andre the Giant in the nads.

- Get a potato with those white things growing out of it. Then put it in the toilet and tell everyone it's a giant alien turd with tentacles.

- And um, I guess you can eat them, but they're not very good. I tried it once. Maybe you hafta cook them or something.

Cool Town Names:
Bonners Ferry
Butte City
Benewah
Peck
Picabo
Standrod

COLORADO

Back in the old days, a bunch of minors went to Colorado cuz there was supposed to be a bunch of gold in the mountains. It's too bad Beavis wasn't around back then, cuz he's real good at digging for gold. Huh huh huh.

Cool Town Names:
Dinosaur
Stoner
Sawpit
Beaver Creek
Wetmore
Two Buttes
Woodrow
Last Chance
Lay

John Denver

DENVER WAS A REALLY COOL CITY, BUT THEN THIS WUSS HAD TO RUIN IT.
WHOA, REALLY? WHAT DID HE DO?
JUST LOOK AT HIM. HUH HUH.

Skiing/ The Rocky Mountains

SKIING COSTS A LOT OF MONEY, SO WE DON'T KNOW ABOUT THAT. BUT IT LOOKS COOL. HUH HUH.

UMMM... I GUESS THE WHOLE POINT OF SKIING IS TO GO DOWN THE HILL AS FAST AS YOU CAN, SO YOU CAN MAKE A REALLY COOL WIPEOUT. HEH HEH. AND UM, THE BETTER YOUR WIPEOUT LOOKS, THE BETTER CHANCE YOU HAVE OF A CHICK COMING UP TO YOU AND ASKING IF YOU'RE OKAY. HEH HEH HEH.

YEAH. HUH HUH. AND IF SHE'S HOT, YOU CAN ASK HER TO TAKE YOU BACK TO YOUR ROOM AND DO IT. YOU KNOW, TO SEE IF YOU'RE REALLY OKAY. UH HUH HUH HUH.

MONTANA

Cool Town Names:
Butte
Four Buttes
Square Butte
Big Timber
Big Arm
Lone Pine
Lodgepole
Goldcreek
Intake
Hungry Horse
Lame Deer
Rocky Boy
Rocker

Joe Montana

WYOMING

Cool Town Names:
Big Piney
Baggs
Meeteetse
Pahaska Teepee
Point of Rocks
Pitchfork
Woods Landing
Chugwater
Smoot

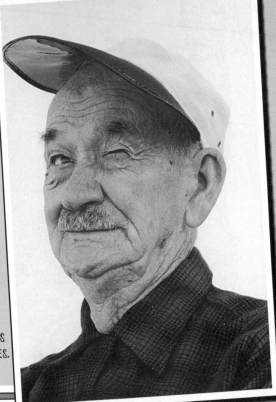

Joe Wyoming

BOTH OF THESE DUDES ARE FAMOUS FOR MAKING PASSES.

YELLOWSTONE

Uh, I guess this is supposed to be a national park or something, but it's like, what the hell is the big deal? Yellowstone sucks.

Yeah, really. I mean, the least they could do is put a brown stone next to it. Heh heh. It's like, that would make it a little better. Heh heh.

Yeah, that would make it better. Huh huh. In fact, I might even go there if they had that. Huh huh huh.

Yeah, me too. Heh heh.

THE GRAND TETONS

TETONS. HUH HUH. WHOEVER NAMED THIS PLACE MUST'VE BEEN REALLY HORNY. HUH HUH.

YEAH, REALLY. HEH HEH. HE WAS PROBABLY TRAVELING ALL AROUND AND HADN'T SEEN CHICKS IN LIKE, YEARS OR SOMETHING. AND THEN WHEN HE SAW THESE BIG MOUNTAINS, HE THOUGHT THEY WERE GIGANTIC BOOBS. HEH HEH HEH.

YEAH, HUH HUH. AND THEN HE GAVE COOL NAMES TO ALL THE OTHER STUFF, TOO. CHECK IT OUT.

The Grand Tetons are located near the Snake River, which runs through Jackson Hole, near Leigh Lake.

States in the Middle

NORTH DUHKOTA

CHECK IT OUT. THERE'S THIS MOVIE, "FARGO," AND IT'S ABOUT THIS PLACE IN NORTH DUHKOTA THAT'S ALL COLD AND COVERED WITH SNOW AND STUFF. BUT THIS PLACE IS COOL, CUZ THEIR COP IS A PREGNANT CHICK. HUH HUH HUH.

WHOA, REALLY? SO YOU MEAN SHE LIKES TO DO IT? HEH HEH.

YEAH, HUH HUH.

Cool Town Names:
Cannon Ball
Butte
Grassy Butte
Dickey
Flasher
Lostwood
Underwood
Pick City
Zap

SOUTH DUHKOTA

HEY BEAVIS, CHECK IT OUT, THERE'S A BUNCH OF TOWNS NAMED AFTER BUTTES IN SOUTH DUHKOTA. HUH HUH HUH. LIKE, BEAR BUTTE.

YEAH, YEAH. WHITE BUTTE. HEH HEH.

THUNDER BUTTE. HUH HUH HUH.

MUD BUTTE. HEH HEH HEH. PLOP!

Cool Town Names:
Eagle Butte
Deadwood
Whitewood
Greenwood
Hidden Timer
Lodgepole
Wakpala
Wounded Knee
Glad Valley
Gayville

MOUNT RUSHMORE

THIS STATUE IS PRETTY COOL, BUT IT'S LIKE, THEY SHOULD'VE FINISHED IT AND CARVED THE REST OF THEIR BODIES.

YEAH, REALLY. IT LOOKS LIKE THEY JUST GOT LAZY. HEH HEH.

HEY BEAVIS, WE SHOULD GO THERE AND CARVE OUR FACES IN THE ROCK. HUH HUH HUH.

YEAH, HEH HEH. AND THEN WE COULD CARVE IT ALL THE WAY DOWN TO OUR SCHLONGS. HEH HEH.

YEAH, HUH HUH. AND WE COULD CARVE REALLY LITTLE SCHLONGS ON THOSE PRESIDENT DUDES. HUH HUH HUH.

MINNESODA

HUH HUH HUH HUH. HEY BEAVIS, CHECK IT OUT. IT'S THE WUSS FORMERLY KNOWN AS PRINCE.

YEAH, HEH HEH. PRIIII-IIINNNCCCE! HEH HEH. IT'S LIKE, HIS NAME ISN'T EVEN PRINCE ANYMORE. IT'S JUST THAT STUPID SYMBOL.

YEAH, WHAT THE HELL IS THAT THING? IT KINDA LOOKS LIKE SOMETHING YOU'D SEE ON A BATHROOM FOR PEOPLE THAT ARE HALF-GUYS AND HALF-CHICKS.

YEAH, REALLY. HEH HEH. AND HALF-WUSS.

I BET HE JUST WENT TO ONE OF THOSE GUYS IN THE MALL WITH A WOODEN CART, AND PAID HIM LIKE FIVE BUCKS TO MAKE THAT SYMBOL. HUH HUH.

YEAH, HEH HEH. WE SHOULD DO THAT. BUT AT LEAST OURS WOULD BE COOL. HEH HEH.

Cool Town Names:
- Embarrass
- Nimrod
- Castle Danger
- Big Woods
- Greenbush
- Hardwick
- Mounds View
- Two Inlets
- Pokegama
- Minnewawa
- Shakopee

Where Prince probly bought his symbol →

The Mall of America in Bloomington, Minnesota. The world's largest enclosed shopping mall.

CANADUH The Big State at the Top

CANADUH DUDES TALK FUNNY, HUH HUH. IT'S LIKE, THEY ALWAYS END SENTENCES WITH "EH," HUH HUH.

YEAH, HEH HEH. THAT'S SOUNDS STUPID, HEH HEH.

YEAH, REALLY. HUH HUH.

HOCKEY IS COOL. HEH HEH.

YEAH. IT'S LIKE, NORMALLY ICE SKATING IS FOR WUSSES. BUT IN ORDER TO PROVE THAT THEY'RE NOT WUSSES, THESE GUYS ARE ALWAYS GETTING INTO FIGHTS AND KICKING EACH OTHER'S ASSES. HUH HUH HUH.

YEAH, YEAH. AND EACH TEAM GETS ONE OF THOSE JASONS FROM FRIDAY THE 13TH, AND EVERYBODY KEEPS SHOOTING STUFF AT HIM AND ONE OF THESE TIMES HE'S GONNA GET PISSED AND TAKE OFF HIS SKATE AND KILL SOMEONE. HEH HEH HEH. IT'S GONNA BE COOL.

IOWUH

THERE'S THIS PLACE IN IOWUH WHERE THAT KEVIN COSTNER DUDE USED TO LIVE. AND IT'S LIKE, A VOICE TOLD HIM, "IF YOU BUILD IT, THEY WILL COME." SO LIKE, HE BUILT A BASEBALL FIELD.

WHAT A DUMBASS. HE SHOULD HAVE BUILT A BED.

YEAH, REALLY. THAT WAY CHICKS WOULD'VE COME FROM ALL OVER. HUH HUH.

OLD PEOPLE, HUH HUH HUH.

MERYL
STREEP
WHOA! CHECK IT OUT.
IT'S THAT CHICK THAT DID IT
WITH CLINT EASTWOOD.
HEH HEH.
WE SHOULD VISIT HER,
CUZ SHE LIKE, LIVES ON THIS
FARM, AND SHE'S ALL LONELY
AND HORNY. HUH HUH HUH.

NUHBRASKA

THERE'S THIS THING IN NUHBRASKA CALLED CARHENGE. IT'S WHERE THIS DUDE TOOK A BUNCH OF CARS AND PAINTED THEM GRAY AND THEN STUCK 'EM IN THE GROUND. AND IT KINDA LOOKS LIKE THAT THING, STONEHENGE, ONLY THIS IS A LOT COOLER.

YEAH, REALLY. STONEHENGE IS JUST A BUNCH OF ROCKS AND NOBODY EVEN KNOWS WHY THEY'RE THERE. AT LEAST THIS MAKES SENSE. HEH HEH.

Cool Town Names:
Beaver Crossing
Surprise
Gross
Butte
Colon
Dix
Long Pine

KANSASS

KANSASS IS WHERE THIS CHICK DOROTHY LIVED WITH HER DOG SCROTO. HUH HUH.

OHHH YEAH, HEH HEH. AND THEN LIKE, A TORNADO CAME AND TOOK HER AWAY TO THIS REALLY WEIRD LAND WHERE ALL THESE LITTLE BUTT-MUNCHKINS TRIED LOOK UP HER DRESS. THOSE GUYS WERE COOL. HEH HEH.

YEAH. HUH HUH. AND THEN THE WICKED BITCH TRIED STEALING HER SHOES. BUT LIKE, ALL DOROTHY WANTED TO DO WAS MEET OZZY. BUT WHEN SHE FINALLY MET HIM, IT WAS JUST SOME OLD DUDE BEHIND A CURTAIN. I BET HE DIDN'T EVEN KNOW ANY BLACK SABBATH SONGS.

YEAH, REALLY. IF IT WAS THE REAL OZZY, HE WOULD'VE BIT THE HEAD OFF OF ONE OF THOSE FLYING MONKEYS. HEH HEH HEH.

YEAH. THAT WOULD'VE BEEN COOL.

Cool Town Names:
Gas
Athol
Beaver
Teterville
Woods
Peck
Protection
Studley
Climax
Wagstaff

Missouri

If you're ever in St. Louis and you're hungry, they have this really big McDonald's there.

Yeah. It's like, really tough to miss, because there's this huge arch that goes over the river.

But uh, the day we were there, I think they were out of food or something, cuz the dude just stared at me like I was a dumbass.

Cool Town Names:
Couch
Devils Elbow
Tightwad
Humansville
Vulcan
Grassy
Brownwood
Dogwood
Pilot Knob
Knob Lick

UH, I'D LIKE A QUARTER POUNDER WITH CHEESE.

MONUMENT TICKETS

OKLUHOMA

SUMMER IS A REALLY COOL TIME TO GO TO OKLUHOMA, CUZ THEY GET A LOT OF TORNADOES. HEH HEH.

TORNADOES ARE COOL, CUZ THEY CAN LIKE, REALLY ADD SOME EXCITEMENT TO YOUR VACATION. HUH HUH.

YEAH, LIKE ONE TIME WHEN I WAS LITTLE, A TORNADO WAS COMING, AND THE WIND WAS REALLY STRONG AND IT GAVE ME A STIFFY. HEH HEH HEH.

BEAVIS, I WISH THAT TORNADO WOULD RIPPED OFF YOUR SCH-LONG. HUH HUH HUH.

THAT'S NOT FUNNY, BUTT-HEAD. HEH HEH. IT'S LIKE, I HEARD THAT TORNADOES CAN PICK UP A COW AND THROW IT THROUGH A FENCE OR SOMETHING. HEH HEH.

REALLY? I ONCE HEARD THAT TORNADOES CAN PICK UP AN ENTIRE HOUSE AND A SEMI-TRUCK AND THROW THAT THROUGH A FENCE. HUH HUH HUH.

WHOA, HEH HEH. IF I LIVED IN OKLUHOMA, I'D PUT UP FENCES EVERYWHERE. HEH HEH. THAT WOULD BE COOL.

Cool Town Names:
Dill City
Jacktown
Hooker
Hogshooter
North Pole
Cox City
Happyland
Gay
Rubottom
Atwood
Bushyhead
Box

TEXASS

TEXASS HAS ALL THESE COWBOYS WHO LIKE, DO WHATEVER THEY WANT, AND THEY LIKE, GO INTO BARS AND START FIGHTS AND BREAK THE LAW AND STUFF.

YEAH. AND SOMETIMES THEY EVEN PLAY FOOTBALL. HEH HEH.

YEAH. AND THEY'VE GOT REALLY HOT CHEERLEADERS, TOO. HUH HUH.

Cool Town Names:
Twin Sisters
Lovelady
Pettus
Round Mountain
Big Thicket
Cheek
Study Butte
Bangs
Brownwood
Quicksand
Woodrow
Camp Wood
Hurlwood
Johnson
Shafter
Pumpville
Deadwood
Slocum
Pluck
Leakey
Gun Barrel City
Happy
Jolly
Joy

DON'T MESS WITH TEXASS

ME AND BEAVIS HEARD ABOUT THIS COOL PORN MOVIE CALLED "DEBBIE DOES DALLAS," SO LIKE, WE WATCHED THIS OLD T.V. SHOW, BUT THERE WASN'T ANY PORN OR NUDITY OR ANYTHING. IT SUCKED. ALL EVERYONE WORRIED ABOUT WAS, WHO SHOT SOME DUMBASS NAMED J.R.?

YEAH, REALLY, IT'S LIKE, WHO THE HELL CARES? I WANNA SEE BOOBS! HEH HEH. DAMMIT!

ARKANSAW

ARKANSAW IS WHERE PEOPLE NAMED BILL COME FROM. LIKE THAT PRESIDENT DUDE.

OH YEAH. HEH HEH. AND THIS OTHER DUDE, BILLY BOB. HE LIKE, TALKS REAL FUNNY, BUT HE'S REALLY SMART AND HE KILLED DWIGHT YOAKAM. I GUESS HE DIDN'T LIKE COUNTRY MUSIC OR SOMETHING. HEH HEH.

Cool Town Names:
Bald Knob
Blue Ball
Weiner
Dogwood
Dogpatch
Hooker
Smackover
Flippin
Lake Dick
Cherry Valley
Wild Cherry
"Y" City
Mounds
Nimrod
Knob
Beverage Town
Seaton Dump

I like the way you laugh. Mm-hmm.

UM, HEH HEH, THANKS. COULD YOU TELL ME AGAIN ABOUT THOSE PEOPLE YOU KILLED? HEH HEH HEH.

LOUISIANUH

LOUISIANUH IS COOL, CUZ EVERYBODY PRACTICES VOODOO IN ORDER TO GET STUFF AND LIKE, WARD OFF EVIL SPIRITS OR SOMETHING.

ONE TIME I HAD AN EVIL SPIRIT UP MY BUTT. HEH HEH. IT WAS MAKING ALL THESE REALLY WEIRD NOISES AND I THINK IT WAS POSSESSED BY THE DEVIL OR SOMETHING. SO LIKE, I HAD TO USE VOODOO TO FIX MY POOPOO. HEH HEH HEH.

OH YEAH, HUH HUH. YOU WERE ON THE TOILET AND YOU WERE SCREAMING. HUH HUH HUH.

YEAH, HEH HEH. SO LIKE, I MADE A MAGIC POTION WITH TABASCO SAUCE, OLD MILK AND TOILET WATER. HEH HEH. THEN I POOPED OUT THE EVIL SPIRIT.

IT SURE SMELLED LIKE AN EVIL SPIRIT. HUH HUH.

YEAH. MY BUTT'S A LOT BETTER NOW. HEH HEH. THANK YOU VERY MUCH.

Cool Town Names:
- Grand Cane
- Grosse Tete
- Kickapoo
- Gassoway
- Hardwood
- Good Pine
- Peck
- Ball
- Belcher
- Cut Off

CHECK IT OUT, IT'S THAT DON DELUISE DUDE.

OHHH YEAH. REMEMBER LIKE, WHEN HE WAS ALL COOL AND STUFF AND HE USED TO HANG OUT WITH BURT REYNOLDS?

YEAH. BUT NOW ALL HE DOES IS COOK FOOD ON T.V. AND GET FAT. HUH HUH HUH.

IT'S KINDA SAD, REALLY. GETTING OLD MUST SUCK. HEH HEH.

Cool Cities – New Orlins

THEY CALL NEW ORLINS THE BIG EASY, CUZ THEY HAVE THIS BIG PARTY CALLED MARTY GRA, WHERE EVERYBODY GETS REALLY DRUNK, AND IF YOU GIVE A CHICK ONE OF THESE CHEAP NECKLACES, SHE'LL SHOW YOU HER BOOBS. HUH HUH HUH.

WHOA, HEH HEH. THOSE CHICKS DO SOUND PRETTY EASY. HEH HEH.

YEAH, HUH HUH. TOO BAD IT'S ONLY ONCE A YEAR. CUZ LIKE, GETTING TO SEE CHICKS' BOOBS SHOULD BE THAT EASY ALL THE TIME. HUH HUH.

Vacation Tips

BUYING SOUVENIRS

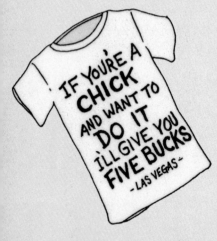

SOUVENIRS SUCK. THEY'RE JUST LIKE REALLY CHEAP CRAP THAT NOBODY EVEN WANTS.

YEAH. IT'S LIKE, NO MATTER HOW STUPID IT IS, SOME DUMBASS IS GONNA BUY IT. HUH HUH.

YEAH, REALLY. THEY NEED TO MAKE SOME COOL STUFF THAT YOU AND ME WOULD BUY. HEH HEH HEH.

ALABAMUH

HEY BEAVIS, DIDN'T YOUR MOM USED TO DO IT WITH SOME DUDE FROM ALABAMUH? HUH HUH. OHHHH YEAH. HEH HEH. THAT BAND SUCKED. HEH HEH.

Misisipi

HEY BUTT-HEAD, ISN'T MISISIPI WHERE THOSE TWO KIDS WENT ACROSS THE LAKE IN A RAFT OR SOMETHING AND HAD ALL THOSE COOL ADVENTURES AND STUFF?

UHHH... OH YEAH. BUT I THINK THAT WAS LIKE, A MOVIE OR SOMETHING.

CUZ WE SHOULD GO THERE AND RENT A RAFT AND HAVE SOME ADVENTURES, TOO. HEH HEH.

WHY THE HELL WOULD WE WANT TO GO SPEND MONEY ON A RAFT WHEN WE CAN SIT HERE AND WATCH ADVENTURES ON T.V. FOR FREE?! THAT WOULD BE LIKE, A BIG WASTE OF MONEY.

OH YEAH, HEH HEH. SORRY ABOUT THAT.

KENTUCKY

UH, I THINK KENTUCKY IS WHERE THAT OLD DUDE MADE CHICKEN.

OHHH YEAH. HEH HEH. UM, HEY BUTT-HEAD, I KNOW WHAT HIS SECRET RECIPE IS. HEH HEH. HE CHOKES HIS CHICKEN. HEH HEH HEH HEH.

BEAVIS, YOU NEED PROFESSIONAL HELP. HUH HUH.

Cool Town Names:
Monkey's Eyebrow
Head of Grassy
Drip Rock
Mammoth Cave
Big Bone
Black Snake
Avawam
Fisty
Athol
Moon
Mud Lick
Clover Bottom
Virgie
Brodhead
Cox's Creek
Stamping Ground

The Kentucky Derby is like, this famous horse race. It's like, all these midgets ride horses and rich people bet money on them. And uh, I guess the winner gets to keep the midget. Huh huh huh.

TENESEE

Cool Town Names:
Bone Cave
Big Lick
Stainville
Big Sandy
Bucksnort
Cherry
Cherry Valley
Finger
Leapwood
Peters Landing
Rockwood
Skullbone
South Tunnel
Gassaway
Woodbury
Frog Jump
Grassy Cove
Hanging Limb
Nutbush
Happy Valley
Hickey
Mount View
Nankipoo

THERE'S THIS PLACE, NASHVILLE, WHERE ALL THEY DO IS DANCE AND LISTEN TO THAT DAMN COUNTRY MUSIC CRAP. HUH HUH.

YEAH, BUT THEY ALSO MAKE WHISKEY IN TENESEE. HEH HEH.

UHHH... OH YEAH. THAT WAY PEOPLE CAN GET ALL DRUNK AND STUFF. CUZ WHEN YOU'RE DRUNK, COUNTRY MUSIC DOESN'T SOUND SO BAD. HUH HUH HUH.

YEAH. AND CHICKS START LOOKING BETTER, TOO. HEH HEH.

YEAH, HUH HUH. YOU KNOW, NASHVILLE IS STARTING TO SOUND PRETTY COOL. HUH HUH HUH.

People You Should Visit

PRISCILLA PRESLEY

WHOA! CHECK IT OUT. IT'S THAT CHICK THAT DID IT WITH ELVIS. HEH HEH.

WE SHOULD VISIT HER, CUZ SHE LIVES ALL ALONE IN THIS BIG HOUSE CALLED GRACELAND, AND SHE'S LIKE, ALL LONELY AND HORNY. HUH HUH HUH. BUT UH, THE ONLY THING THAT SUCKS IS, THE WHOLE DAMN HOUSE IS FILLED WITH CRAP ABOUT ELVIS.

Cool Cities – Chicago

Chicago is called "The Windy City." Huh huh.

Whoa, really? It must smell pretty bad. Heh heh. Poop.

You dumbass. Huh huh. It's cool, cuz the wind blows up all the chicks dresses and you get to see their underwear. Huh huh huh. That's why those weather-dudes are always calling it a stiff breeze. Uh huh huh huh.

Oprah's pretty smart, cuz like, every year she gets really fat and then she loses a whole bunch of weight and everybody's like, "Whoa. How'd she do it? She looks great!" Huh huh huh.

Yeah, yeah. And then she's like, "Oh, like, thanks for noticing. Heh heh. I just wrote a book about it. And you can buy it for like, thirty dollars." Heh heh heh.

Yeah, and then she gets a whole bunch of money and starts eating again. Huh huh huh.

ILLiNOY Land of Lincoln

CHECK IT OUT, IT'S THAT DUDE WHO INVENTED THE PENNY.

SO WHAT? PENNIES ARE WORTHLESS. HEH HEH.

YEAH. HUH HUH. HE MUST'VE FIGURED OUT THAT PENNIES SUCK, CUZ HE ALSO INVENTED THE FIVE DOLLAR BILL. HUH HUH.

YEAH, BUT THEN SOMEBODY ELSE CAME ALONG AND INVENTED THE TEN DOLLAR BILL AND THEN THE HUNDRED DOLLAR BILL AND NOW IT DOESN'T LOOK LIKE SUCH A BIG DEAL. HEH HEH.

YEAH, REALLY. HE COULD'VE DONE LIKE, SO MUCH MORE WITH HIS LIFE. HUH HUH HUH.

INDIANA Land of Letterman

LETTERMAN IS COOL. HUH HUH.

YEAH, YEAH. INDIANA MUST BE REALLY PROUD OF HIM. HEH HEH.

YEAH. THEY PROBABLY HAVE THOSE HYSTERICAL MARKERS UP EVERYWHERE, SAYING STUFF LIKE, "THIS IS WHERE DAVE SLEPT." HUH HUH.

HEH HEH. AND "THIS IS WHERE DAVE SLEPT WITH A CHICK." HEH HEH HEH.

AND "THIS IS WHERE DAVE'S MOM KICKED HIM OUT OF THE HOUSE AND SAID, "DON'T EVER BRING THAT SLUT AROUND HERE AGAIN!"" HUH HUH HUH.

YEAH, YEAH! "AND I'M SICK OF YOU LYING AROUND, WATCHING THAT DUMBASS JOHNNY CARSON. WHY DON'T YOU GET YOUR OWN DAMN T.V. SHOW IF YOU THINK YOU'RE SO FUNNY!" HEH HEH HEH.

DAVE'S MOM IS COOL. HUH HUH HUH.

Cool Town Names:
Floyds Knobs
Bushrod
Easytown
Cumback
French Lick
Dogwood
Beaver City
Gas City
Aroma
Gnaw Bone
Old Bath
Spraytown

Indianapolis 500

Whoa! Multiple car pile-up! Yeaaah! Heh Heh. Arrrrgggghhhh!

OHIO

HEY BUTT-HEAD, CHECK IT OUT, THERE'S A TOWN IN OHIO WITH THE SAME NAME AS ME. HEH HEH.

REALLY? YOU MEAN BUTTKNOCKER? HUH HUH HUH.

Cool Town Names:
Bevis
Bangs
Cherry Valley
Climax
Delightful
Blue Ball
Crooked Tree
Conesville
Long Bottom
Chickasaw
Getaway
Flushing
Fly

WELCOME TO BEVIS

The first artificial heart is on display at The Museum of the International Center for Artificial Organs and Transplantation, located in Cleveland.

Hey Beavis, you should go to this place and ask for an artificial schlong.

Cool Cities - CLEVELAND

THE COOLEST THING ABOUT CLEVELAND IS THIS RIVER. LIKE, IN THE 70'S IT WAS ALL POLLUTED AND STUFF AND IT WAS ON FIRE. HUH HUH HUH.

WHOA, HEH HEH. THEY SHOULD DO THAT AGAIN. CUZ THAT'S SOMETHING I'D REALLY LIKE TO SEE. HEH HEH HEH.

CLEVELAND HAS THIS PLACE CALLED THE ROCK AND ROLL HALL OF FAME, BUT IT'S NOT AS COOL AS IT SOUNDS. IT'S LIKE, THE ONLY BANDS THAT ARE IN THERE ARE EITHER DEAD OR THEY PLAY MUSIC THAT NOBODY LISTENS TO ANYMORE. HUH HUH.

YEAH. IT'S LIKE, THEY PICK ALL THOSE OLD BANDS CUZ EVERYBODY FEELS SORRY FOR THEM. HEH HEH.

MiSHiGAN

MiSHiGAN iS WHERE CARS ARE MADE. AND PRiSON iS WHERE LiCENSE PLATES ARE MADE. HEH HEH.

YEAH. SO iF YOU GET BORED ON YOUR VACATiON, A COOL THiNG TO DO iS CHECK OUT PEOPLE'S LiCENSE PLATES AND TRY TO FiGURE OUT WHAT THEY SAY. CUZ iT COULD BE A MESSAGE FROM THE DUDES iN PRiSON.

YEAH. BUT MOST LiCENSE PLATES SUCK. THEY JUST HAVE A BUNCH OF NUMBERS AND LETTERS THAT DON'T MAKE ANY SENSE. SO LiKE, HERE ARE SOME COOL LiCENSE PLATES THAT ME AND BUTT-HEAD ARE GONNA MAKE SOMEDAY. HEH HEH. YOU KNOW, iF WE EVER GET THE CHANCE.

Cool Town Names:
Nirvana
Hell
Bad Axe
Peck
Jugville
Point Nipigon
Clam River
Woodhaven
Needmore

DR. DEATH

THIS DUDE IS COOL. HIS NAME IS "DR. DEATH." I THINK HE'S LIKE A PRO WRESTLER OR SOMETHING. BUT HE WEARS ONE OF THOSE MASKS WHEN HE'S IN THE RING, YOU KNOW, TO DISGUISE HIS HEAD. HUH HUH.

HE DOESN'T LOOK THAT STRONG, BUT I HEARD HE'S GOT A KILLER SLEEPER HOLD. HEH HEH HEH.

WISCONSIN

WISCONSIN IS WHERE THEY MAKE A LOT OF BEER AND CHEESE. AND IT'S LIKE, THE PEOPLE DRINK SO MUCH BEER THAT THEY DON'T KNOW WHAT THE HELL IS GOING ON AND THEY CAN'T FIND THEIR HATS AND STUFF. SO THEY JUST GRAB SOME CHEESE AND PUT IT ON THEIR HEADS. HUH HUH HUH.

WHOA, THAT'S COOL. CUZ WHEN SUMMER COMES, THE CHEESE WOULD MELT AND YOU COULD MAKE NACHOS ON YOUR HEAD. HEH HEH HEH.

Cool Town Names:
Spread Eagle
Sugar Bush
Big Patch
Pound
Cream
Pipe
Beaver Dam
Butternut
Hustler
Woodman
Clam Falls

CHECK IT OUT. A LONG TIME AGO, LIKE WHEN RON HOWARD STILL HAD HAIR, PEOPLE THOUGHT THAT FONZIE DUDE WAS REALLY COOL. HUH HUH HUH.

YEAH, HEH HEH. HE WOULD SNAP HIS FINGERS AND CHICKS WOULD COME UP TO HIM AND THEY WOULD DO IT. HEH HEH HEH.

I GUESS CHICKS WERE REALLY EASY BACK THEN. HUH HUH.

YEAH, HEH HEH. HAPPY DAYS.

Vacation Tips

SEASONAL TEMPERATURES AND WEATHER

WHEN YOU GO ON VACATION, DON'T GO WHERE THE WEATHER SUCKS.

Winter

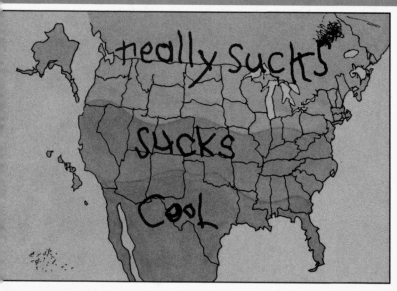

Summer

ME AND BEAVIS WANTED A PET, SO WE WENT TO THE GROCERY STORE, CUZ THEY WERE SELLING THESE COOL LIVE LOBSTERS. HUH HUH.

YEAH. AND THE DUDE BEHIND THE COUNTER SAID THEY WERE FROM MAIN. HEH HEH.

AND LIKE, AFTER HE TOOK THE LOBSTER OUT OF THE AQUARIUM, HE TOLD US TO TAKE IT HOME AND PUT IT IN BOILING WATER. HUH HUH.

YEAH, HEH HEH. THAT DUDE WAS COOL. SO WE THREW THE LOBSTER IN SOME BOILING WATER AND THEN IT SCREAMED AND DIED. IT WAS PRETTY FUN. HEH HEH.

YEAH, HUH HUH. I BET THAT'S WHAT PEOPLE IN MAIN DO FOR A GOOD TIME.

Stephen King

This dude is scary. He probably started all that lobster stuff. huh huh.

Cool Town Names:
Todd's Corner
Mechanic Falls
Lookout
Head Tide
Greenbush
Dickey
Bald Head
Small Point
Meddybemps
Bowdoinham
Passadumkeag

NEW HAMPSURE

Cool Town Names:
Penacook
Ossipee
Sunapee
Cones
Twin Mountain
Bath
Woodman
Exeter
Sandwich
Center Sandwich
Dummer

THIS IS THE STATE
THAT LOOKS LIKE VERMONT.
UHHH, WAIT. MAYBE THIS IS
VERMONT.

VERMONT

Cool Town Names:
Barre
Vergennes
Hardwick
Shaftsbury
Middlesex
Bread Loaf
Pompanoosuc

VERMONT
IS LIKE, WHERE
THOSE TWO OLD
FAT HIPPIES MAKE
ICE CREAM. AND
THEY JUST LIKE, SIT
AROUND AND THINK OF
STUPID NAMES FOR THEIR ICE
CREAM. HUH HUH.

YEAH, HEH HEH. THEY LIKE, NEED SOME BETTER NAMES FOR THEIR ICE
CREAM, LIKE CHUNKY BUTT-MONKEY. DINGLEBERRY GARCIA. HEH HEH.
CHOCOLATE CHIP POOPIE DOUGH. HEH HEH HEH.

SETTLE DOWN, BEAVIS. HUH HUH.

State Mottos

EVERY STATE HAS ONE OF THESE THINGS CALLED A "MOTTO." IT'S KINDA LIKE ADVERTISING, ONLY THEY CAME UP WITH THESE A LONG TIME AGO AND THEY ALL SUCK. SO ME AND BEAVIS CAME UP WITH SOME BETTER ONES.

State:	Motto:	What the motto should be:
Airizona	God Enriches	DEAR GOD, I NEED MONEY
Alabamuh	We Dare Defend Our Rights	DON'T MAKE US KICK YOUR ASS
Alaskuh	North to the Future	SOUTH TO THE WARM WEATHER
Arkansaw	The People Rule	THE PEEP-HOLE RULES
Huhwaii	The Life of the Land Is Perpetuated in Righteousness	GET LEIGHED
Iowuh	Our Liberties We Prize and Our Rights We Will Maintain	WIN FABULOUS PRIZES!
Kansass	To the Stars Through Difficulties	WE'RE ALL GONNA DIE AND GO TO HEAVEN
Maryland	Manly Deeds, Womanly Words	DUDES DO. CHICKS TALK.
Mishigan	If You See a Pleasant Peninsula, Look About You	IF YOU SEE A BIG SCHLONG, IT'S MINE
Missouri	Let the Welfare of the People Be the Supreme Law	EVERYONE SHOULD BE ON WELFARE
Montana	Oro y Plata	GET ME A PLATE OF OREOS
Nebraska	Equality Before the Law	SCREW THE LAW
Nevaduh	Battle Born	FIGHT, FIGHT, FIGHT!!!
New Hampsure	Live Free or Die	POOP OR DIE
New Mexico	It Grows as it Goes	IT GETS STIFF WHEN I PEE
North Carolina	To Be Rather Than to Seem	BE COOL, NOT A WUSS
Oklahoma	Labor Conquers All Things	WORK SUCKS
Oregon	She Flies With Her Own Wings	FLIES ARE COOL
South Duhkota	Great Faces, Great Places	HEY BABY, NICE THINGEES
Washingtun	By-and-by	SEE YA LATER
West Virginya	Mountaineers Are Always Free	MOUNTAINEERS ARE NAKED

MASACHOOSETS

BOSTON IS COOL, CUZ EVERYBODY JUST HANGS OUT IN A BAR AND DRINKS ALL DAY. BUT IT'S WEIRD, CUZ EVERYONE KNOWS YOUR NAME.

WHOA, HEH HEH. SO LIKE, IF I JUST WALKED IN, EVERYONE WOULD KNOW MY NAME?

YEAH. AND THEY'D ALL SHOUT IT OUT AT THE SAME TIME. HUH HUH.

BUT LIKE, DON'T THESE PEOPLE HAVE LIVES OR SOMETHING?

DAMMIT BEAVIS, WHY WOULD YOU WANT A LIFE IF YOU CAN JUST SIT IN A BAR ALL DAY AND WATCH THE BARTENDER TRY TO SCORE WITH A CHICK. HUH HUH.

OHHHH YEAH, HEH HEH. THAT'S A GOOD POINT.

WHERE TO FIND THE HOTTEST CHICKS

CHICKS ARE LIKE, AN ELUSIVE BREED OR SOMETHING. HUH HUH. SO IF YOU WANT TO SCORE WHEN YOU GO ON VACATION, IT WOULD BE COOL TO KNOW WHERE MOST OF THE CHICKS ARE. HUH HUH.

YEAH, YEAH. SO LIKE, WE TORE THIS MAP OUT OF A SCHOOLBOOK. HEH HEH. IT SHOWS WHERE THE MOST PEOPLE LIVE OR SOMETHING.

AND UH, IT'S A PRETTY GOOD BET THAT IF THERE ARE PEOPLE THERE, THERE ARE CHICKS, TOO. HUH HUH HUH.

YEAH. AND THEY'RE PROBABLY ALL HOT AND HORNY AND WAITING FOR YOUR CALL. HEH HEH.

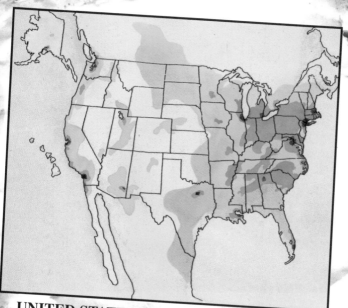

UNITED STATES POPULATION DENSITY

MAP LEGEND

- Sucks. No chicks.
- Okay. Could use more chicks.
- Lotsa chicks here
- Booooiiinnng!!!

CONNETICUT

Cool Town Names:
Mechanicsville
Hazardville
Whigville
Woodville
Packerville
Woodbury
Haddam Neck

WHOA. THIS PLACE LOOKS COOL.

YEAH, YEAH. IT'S LIKE, EVERYTHING I'VE ALWAYS WANTED IN A VACATION. HEH HEH. I COULD SPEND WEEKS THERE.

YEAH. IT LOOKS LIKE A GOOD PLACE FOR KIDS, TOO.

YEAH, REALLY. IT LOOKS LIKE PANTERA JUST PLAYED THERE. HEH HEH.

UHHHH... HEY BEAVIS, ARE YOU SURE THIS IS A PICTURE OF CONNETICUT?

UM, NO. I JUST TORE IT OUT OF A MAGAZINE, CUZ I LIKED IT. HEH HEH.

DAMMIT BEAVIS, YOU GOT MY HOPES UP FOR NOTHING.

OH, UM, SORRY ABOUT THAT. HEH HEH.

ROAD ISLAND

The smallest state, huh huh.

Cool Town Names:
Monkeytown
Nooseneck
Greenwood
Slocum
Quonochontaug
Weekapaug

ROAD ISLAND IS THE SMALLEST STATE. HUH HUH. SO IT'S PROBABLY A GOOD PLACE TO VISIT IF YOU HAVE AN HOUR TO KILL OR SOMETHING.

BUT I BET IT SUCKS IF YOU LIVE IN ROAD ISLAND, CUZ YOU'RE PROBABLY ALWAYS BUMPING INTO THINGS AND OTHER PEOPLE AND STUFF. SO LIKE, HERE'S SOME STUFF THAT THEY SHOULD DO TO MAKE ROAD ISLAND BIGGER:

- Invade Conneticut.

- Use a bunch of those mirrors that make everything look bigger.

- Put cinder blocks under everything to make it taller.

- Late at night, when other states are asleep, they should move their border farther out.

- One time I saw that Martha Stewart chick say that if you took all the furniture out of a room it looked bigger. So, uh, Road Island should get rid of all its furniture.

NEW YORK

THERE'S THIS PLACE WOODSTOCK, WHERE LIKE, A MILLION KIDS WENT OUT IN THIS FIELD AND ROLLED AROUND IN THE MUD AND STUFF. HUH HUH.

YEAH. IT LOOKED PRETTY COOL. HEH HEH. BUT UM, WASN'T THERE SUPPOSED TO BE A CONCERT OR SOMETHING? HEH HEH.

UHHH... I DON'T KNOW. IF THERE WAS, NOBODY PAID ATTENTION.

YEAH. EVERYBODY WAS TOO BUSY TRYING TO SEE BOOBS. HEH HEH.

The Statue of Liberty - A highlight of the visit includes a trip to the inside of her ~~crown~~ butt

Cool Town Names:
Barre Center
Halfmoon
Peekamoose
Lackawack
Little Neck
Inwood
Flatbush
Sparrow Bush
Flushing
Garbutt
Rock Tavern
Rockwood
Tuckahoe
Tunnel
Purchase
Protection
Turnwood
Underwood
Great Kills
Fishkill
Kill Buck
Killawog
Kripplebush
Horseheads

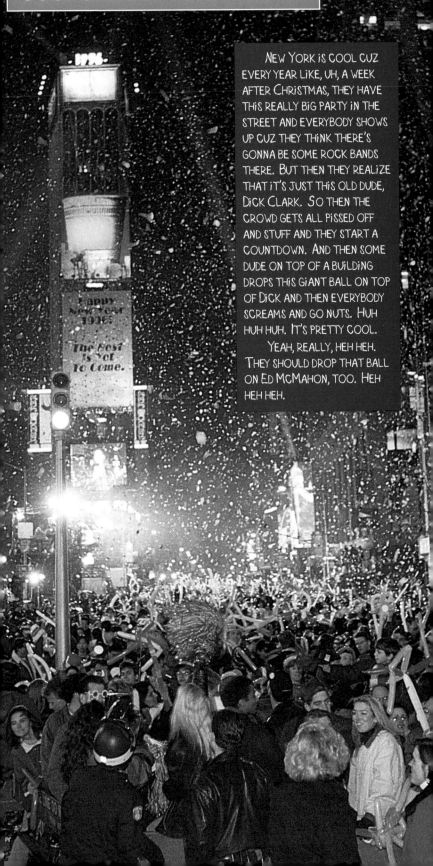

Cool Cities – New York

New York is cool cuz every year like, uh, a week after Christmas, they have this really big party in the street and everybody shows up cuz they think there's gonna be some rock bands there. But then they realize that it's just this old dude, Dick Clark. So then the crowd gets all pissed off and stuff and they start a countdown. And then some dude on top of a building drops this giant ball on top of Dick and then everybody screams and go nuts. Huh huh huh. It's pretty cool.

Yeah, really, heh heh. They should drop that ball on Ed McMahon, too. Heh heh heh.

If you live in New York City, you're probably either a cop or you sit around your apartment with your friends and just talk about stupid stuff. If me and Beavis lived in New York, we'd kick some ass and score.

KRAMER

THIS DUDE IS PRETTY COOL. HE LIKE, LIVES ACROSS THE HALL FROM THAT SEINFELD DUDE AND HE'S ALWAYS GOING OVER THERE AND BORROWING STUFF.

YEAH, HUH HUH. HE SHOULD BORROW SOME OF SEINFELD'S CHICKS. HUH HUH. THEN, WHEN SEINFELD AND THAT GEORGE DUDE ARE TALKING ABOUT ALL THEIR STUPID CRAP, THE CAMERA COULD FOLLOW KRAMER AND THE CHICK BACK TO HIS APARTMENT, CUZ I BET HE KNOWS HOW TO GET CHICKS TO UH, YOU KNOW. UH HUH HUH HUH.

YEAH. THAT WOULD MAKE THE SHOW A LOT BETTER. HEH HEH HEH.

PENSILVANIA

Check it out,
Pensilvania has
more cool town
names than any
other state:
Intercourse
Bareville
Black Lick
Blue Knob
Blue Ball
Balls Mills
Broad Top City
Burnt Cabins
Mars
Metal
Rock
Round Top
Annisville
Ohiopyle
Jollytown
Knobsville
Laboratory
Lickingville
Little Hope
Fairchance
Needful
Needmore
Cherry Valley
Deep Valley
Valley View
Dilltown
Drinker
Dry Tavern
Duff City
Fallen Timber
Gastown
Home
Hometown
Hooker
Porkey
Stewarts Run
Dry Run
Smoke Run
Moon Run
Todd
Torpedo
Wood
Kingwood
Leatherwood
Longwood
Parkwood
Rockwood
Wildwood

Woodbury
Woodcock
Woodrow
Youngwood
Yellow Creek
Big Mount
Big Beaver
Shy Beaver
Bushkill
Butztown
Bird-In-Hand
Energy
Effort
Fearnot
Walnut Bottom
Hop Bottom
Lookout
Pillow
Middlesex
Gap
Little Gap
Wind Gap
Pleasant Gap
Pleasant Valley
Pleasant Hills
Pleasant Mount
Reamstown
Rough and Ready
Virginville

I BET PENSILVANIA IS PRETTY SCARY, SINCE THAT'S LIKE, WHERE VAMPIRES COME FROM.

BEAVIS, YOU DUMBASS, THAT'S TRANSYLVANIA. PENSILVANIA HAS THOSE AMISH DUDES, WHO LIKE, DON'T USE ELECTRICITY OR HAVE T.V.s AND STUFF.

WHOA, HEH HEH. THAT'S EVEN SCARIER.

People You Should Visit

THE AMISH

NEW JERZEE

NEW JERZEE ALWAYS GETS PICKED ON, CUZ SPRINGSTEEN AND BON JOVI ARE FROM THERE. HUH HUH.

YEAH, REALLY. WHY WOULD ANYONE WANT TO GO THERE IF THERE'S A CHANCE YOU'RE GOING TO RUN INTO THESE GUYS? HEH HEH.

YEAH, HUH HUH. CUZ THEY PROBABLY WON'T LEAVE YOU ALONE. THEY'LL LIKE, TAKE YOU EVERYWHERE AND SAY STUFF LIKE, "THIS IS WHERE I GREW UP, AND THIS IS WHERE I WROTE MY FIRST SONG, AND THIS IS WHERE I SCORED WITH A CHICK BACK IN THE 80'S." HUH HUH HUH.

TALK ABOUT A CRAPPY WAY TO RUIN A COOL VACATION. HEH HEH HEH.

Cool Town Names:
Buttzville
Cheesequake
Penny Pot
Pole Tavern
Woods Tavern
Bear Tavern
Double
Trouble
Fort Dix
Highwood
Spotswood
Wildwood
Beachwood
Fanwood
Beaver Run
Middlebush
Tuckahoe
Wickatunk
Ho-Ho-Kus
Leektown
Spray Beach
Little Ferry
Loveladies
Pecks Corner

MARYLAND

CRABS, HUH HUH HUH.

IT'S LIKE, EVERYONE GOES TO MARYLAND TO GET CRABS, BUT UM, ONCE I GOT CRABS FROM THE TOILET SEAT AT THE GAS STATION. HEH HEH. I WAS GONNA EAT THEM, BUT THEY WERE TOO SMALL. HEH HEH.

DELUHWARE

UH, I THINK THIS IS WHERE THAT OLD DUDE, WASHINGTON, CROSSED THE RIVER AND DISCOVERED AMERICA.

Vacation Tips

RESTAURANT GUIDE

What To Look For:

- Places with a lot of pick-up trucks and motorcycles out front.

- If a restaurant doesn't have a drive-thru, forget it. You're s'posed to be traveling. Don't waste your time in some nice restaurant.

- Places that are all run-down with broken windows. The food is usually cheaper.

- Places with a one-star rating. They usually aren't very busy.

- Dumpsters that aren't locked up. Cuz sometimes, at the end of the night, they throw perfectly good food away.

- Restrooms on the outside. Cuz sometimes you just wanna poop.

Tom Anderson's Trip Tips

Here's a few tips to help you relax and enjoy your vacation:

- Always tell relatives where you're going, in case you get abducted.

- Be prepared. Watch the weather reports for at least 3 days prior to leaving.

- Call the automobile association to make sure your membership is in good standing.

- Two spare tires are better than one.

- The most important thing on a camper is a good propane regulator.

- Get a headstart on traffic and make the most of daylight. Be on the road by 5 a.m.

- Plan your bathroom stops to coincide with historical markers.

- Always lock your vehicle.

- Don't use the air conditioner. You might sweat a little, but you'll get better gas mileage.

- Always listen to AM radio. You'll get some local flavor as well as emergency updates.

- Never pick up hitch-hikers. They're probably on drugs and a long walk will do 'em some good.

- Make sure you have fun.

WASHINGTUN D.C.

WASHINGTUN D.C. IS WHERE THE PRESIDENT AND A BUNCH OF OLD DUDES BREAK THE LAWS AND SLEEP WITH CHICKS. HUH HUH. BUT I DON'T THINK THEY EVER GO TO JAIL OR ANYTHING. I GUESS THEY'RE JUST CHECKING TO SEE IF THE LAWS REALLY WORK.

THOSE POLITICIANS ARE A BUNCH OF BUNGHOLES. HEH HEH. IT'S LIKE, THEY'RE ALWAYS TALKING ABOUT HOW THERE'S TOO MUCH VIO-LENCE ON T.V. NO THERE ISN'T! THERE'S TOO MANY TALK-SHOWS WITH WUSSY FARTKNOCKERS WHINING ABOUT THEIR DUMBASS PROBLEMS. IF I WAS ON ONE OF THOSE TALK-SHOWS, I'D SHOW 'EM VIOLENCE. I'D KICK EVERYBODY'S ASS. INCLUDING THE AUDIENCE. YEEEAAAHH! HEH HEH HEH.

Historical Fact: Washingtun D.C. was like, named after America's first president. I guess his last name must've been really stupid or something, and that's why they only use the D.C. part.

VIRGINYA

VIRGINYA, HUH HUH HUH.
YEAH, HEH HEH HEH. BOOOOINNNG!

Uh, I Think There Was a War Around Here Somewhere

by Butt-Head

Once upon a time there was a war. And uh, it was a long time ago, before the United States got cool. Like, a bunch of old dudes from the north and a bunch of old dudes from the south were pissed at each other cuz they both wanted to score with some virgins in Virginya. So they fought in this field somewhere, and I think a couple of dudes died and stuff. But then they realized there were enough chicks to go around, so they agreed to make a country and live happily ever after. With liberty and chicks for all.

The end.

Cool Town Names:
Bumpass
Lahore
Pardee
Todds Tavern
Pounding Mill
Big Rock
Left Hand
Philpott
Gasburg
Burnt
Chimney
Modest Town
Birdsnest

WEST VIRGINYA

Cool Town
Names:
Volcano
Tornado
Burnt House
Fraziers
Bottom
Piney View
Pipestem
Organ Cave
Hanging Rock
Droop
Stumptown
Bald Knob
Looneyville

UHHH... I HAVE NO IDEA WHAT GOES ON HERE.
YEAH, ME NEITHER.

NORTH CAROLINA

Visitors to **Winston-Salem** can witness the entire cigarette manufacturing process, where the factory turns out 300 million cigarettes a day.

WHOA, HEH HEH. I WONDER IF THAT'S WHERE THAT CAMEL DUDE IS FROM. HEH HEH.

IT'S LIKE, THAT CAMEL DUDE IS PRETTY COOL AND STUFF. BUT LIKE, IF HE'S NOT AROUND ANYMORE, I JUST CAN'T SEE WHY ANYONE WOULD WANT TO SMOKE. HUH HUH HUH.

YEAH, REALLY. HEH HEH. IT'S LIKE, THEY'RE ALWAYS SAYING HOW THAT CAMEL IS SELLING CIGARETTES TO KIDS. BUT I USED TO LOOK FOR HIM OUTSIDE OF SCHOOL, AND I NEVER SAW HIM. HEH HEH HEH.

SOUTH CAROLINA

AAAAGGGHHH! IT'S HOOTIE AND THE BLOWFISH! HEH HEH.

I BET A COUPLE OF YEARS AGO, SOUTH CAROLINA WAS LIKE REALLY PROUD OF THOSE GUYS. HUH HUH HUH.

YEAH, HEH HEH HEH. NOW THEY'RE JUST LIKE, "HOOTIE WHO?" HEH HEH.

GEORJUH

ATLANTA IS LIKE, WHERE ALL THE NEWS COMES FROM.

BUT UM, HOW DO THEY KNOW WHAT'S GOING ON IN THE REST OF THE WORLD?

UHHHH, I THINK THEY USE HIDDEN CAMERAS, LIKE ON THAT CANDID CAMERA SHOW.

WHOA, HEH HEH. SO YOU MEAN, IF I'M BEHIND THE SCHOOL, TAKING A DUMP, IT COULD END UP ON THE NEWS?

YEAH, HUH HUH.

WOW. THAT'S PRETTY COOL. HEH HEH. I'M GONNA HAVE TO START WATCHING THE NEWS MORE OFTEN. CUZ I'VE PROBABLY BEEN ON A WHOLE BUNCH OF TIMES WITHOUT EVEN KNOWING IT. HEH HEH.

FLORIDUH

Cool Town Names:
- Miccosukee
- Lacoochee
- Homosassa
- Okahumpka
- Titusville
- Wonderwood
- Johnson
- Big Pine
- Goldenrod
- Dr. Phillips
- Howey in the Hills
- Spuds
- Christmas
- Devils Garden

FLORIDUH IS LIKE, WHERE OLD PEOPLE HAVE TO GO WHEN THEY GET REALLY TIRED. HEH HEH.

IT'S "RETIRED," DUMBASS. HUH HUH. AND IT'S ALSO WHERE COLLEGE KIDS GO FOR SPRING BREAK.

BUT LIKE, WHY DOES EVERYONE GO TO FLORIDUH IF THERE'S JUST A BUNCH OF OLD PEOPLE THERE?

BEAVIS, DON'T YOU KNOW ANYTHING? YOU GO TO FLORIDUH, CUZ YOU WANNA GET NAKED AND PARTY AND STUFF AND OLD PEOPLE ARE TOO SLOW TO CATCH YOU. HUH HUH HUH.

Cool Cities - Miami

This is like, where that show 'The Real World' was done. I guess MTV like, did some scientific research of uh, what makes the world real or something. Huh huh.

Yeah. Take a bunch of whiny white kids and maybe like, one Spanish dude and a black chick. Oh yeah, and a gay dude. Heh heh. And then put 'em in a really nice house and listen to their stupid arguments. Heh heh.

And that's supposed to be America or something. Huh huh.

Yeah, but the show isn't very real. If it was really the real world they would've shown some dude spanking the monkey and a chick taking a dump and stuff. Heh heh heh.

Yeah, really. What the hell were the cameramen doing? They missed all the good stuff. It's like, if I went to Miami, I'd go to this house and knock on the door and say, "Uh, excuse me. I've been watching your show for quite some time now. And uh, you chicks need to get naked and get it on. Huh huh. So like, here I am, baby. Come to Butt-Head." Huh huh huh huh.

THE REAL WORLD

Theme Parks

THEME PARKS KICK ASS! HUH HUH. YOU GET TO EAT COTTON CANDY AND THEN GO ON ROLLERCOASTERS AND RIDES AND STUFF. AND IF YOU'RE LUCKY, YOU GET TO SEE SOMEBODY PUKE. HUH HUH.

YEAH, HEH HEH. EXCEPT I HATE IT WHEN THOSE DAMN PEOPLE IN CARTOON COSTUMES COME UP TO YOU AND ACT ALL HAPPY AND STUFF. THOSE THINGS CREEP ME OUT. IT'S LIKE, THEY JUST STARE AT YOU AND THEY NEVER BLINK. HEH HEH.

BEAVIS, YOU DUMBASS. THEY NEVER BLINK BECAUSE IT'S A COSTUME. HUH HUH.

I KNOW THAT! HEH HEH. IT'S JUST, THEY CREEP ME OUT. AND ONE OF THESE DAYS I'M GONNA RIP THE HEAD OFF ONE OF THOSE THINGS AND THEN I'M GONNA TEAR THE EYES OUT AND SHOVE IT UP ITS BUTT! HEH HEH HEH. I'LL BET THEY BLINK THEN.